Toybox Tales

Written by Graham Marks —— Illustrated by Carole Gray

SIENA

Jack's Surprise

Jack loved being a Jack-in-a-box. He loved springing up out of his box at the most unexpected moments and giving the other toys in the playroom a fright! He loved going "WHEEEEEE!" when the top of the box opened, but most of all he loved bouncing around on his spring and laughing at everyone. Jack was a happy toy indeed.

All the other toys had thought Jack was lots of fun to begin with, but they soon got tired with the top of his box flying open suddenly when they weren't expecting it and seeing Jack bobbing about on his spring grinning at them. So, one night they all agreed that they'd had just about enough of Jack, and had a meeting behind the toy box to decide what to do...

The next morning, when Jack heard someone walk past his box he giggled to himself and undid the catch, ready to spring out and scare them, but nothing

happened! He was stuck in his box and no matter how hard he pushed, he couldn't open the lid. Poor Jack just didn't understand what was going on. Meanwhile, outside the box, all the toys sat around and watched Jack's box. This was because on top of it sat Big Jumbo, the elephant. Jumbo was the biggest and heaviest of all the toys. All the time, inside the box Jack pushed and pushed and pushed...

"Do you think it's about time now?" asked Jumbo quietly, after he'd been sitting on the box for about half an hour. Everyone agreed that it was about time. "I'll jump off just as he pushes really hard!" whispered Jumbo. All the toys held their breath as Jumbo jumped off the box and the lid sprang open - and out of the box leapt Jack, bouncing on his spring. Only this time it was Jack who had a fright as all his friends went "WHEEEE!" and burst into laughter!

Scary Sam's Smile

Each night as it got dark and the stars came out, Scary Sam the inflatable skeleton would wake up. His glow-in-the-dark bones would shine in the darkness of the playroom and all the other toys would shiver and find a place to hide. This made Scary Sam very sad, because he was lonely and he only wanted to play. He didn't mean to look scary, but he was crumpled, saggy and miserable looking, because he wasn't properly blown up.

So poor Sam would sit in the corner all alone every night. Until one night when Sam was wandering in the playroom, and he stepped on a drawing pin that had fallen out of the pin board on the wall. PSSSSSS!...PSSSSSS...PSSSSSS! Sam slowly crumpled into a heap, as all the air escaped from his inflatable body. Big Ted was the first to help, as he wasn't really scared of anything. "What's the trouble?" he asked, kneeling by the floppy skeleton. "I...I...I've got a puncture," gasped Sam, but he hardly had enough air left to speak. Soon Rag Doll and Soldier came to help. "Sticky tape! That's what we need," said Soldier and off he went to find some. Soon he was

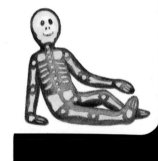

back and a small piece of tape was stuck over the hole made by the pin.

"Now, who's got plenty of puff?" said Soldier, "because we've got to blow him up again. I'll start." Soldier blew into the valve on Sam's back. He blew... and blew...and blew...and blew, and slowly Scary Sam started to grow. When Soldier ran out of puff, Big Ted took over and even Rag Doll took her turn. The more they blew, the bigger Scary Sam got and then something surprising happened...

...Scary Sam's face, which was usually saggy and miserable, began to get a smile, and the more they blew, the bigger the smile got. "That's it," said Soldier, "he's blown right up!" Now Scary Sam had the biggest smile in the playroom, and no one was ever scared of him again.

The Smartest Soldier

from the dolls and soft toys. "Left, right, left, right!" he would shout out as he marched along. "About turn!"

But over the years Soldier Bob had been taken into the garden by the children, where they threw him into bushes, buried him in the ground and tied him onto handkerchief parachutes and dropped him out of the trees. After being treated like this for a while, Soldier Bob wasn't a very happy soldier. His lovely red jacket was torn and muddy, his trousers were so dirty that you could hardly see the yellow

When Soldier Bob had arrived in the playroom he'd been the smartest toy in the toy box - beautiful red jacket, trousers with yellow stripes down the sides, shiny black shoes and a tall black hat set at a jaunty angle on his head.

To begin with he'd marched proudly up and down the playroom, enjoying all the admiring glances he was getting stripes, and his shiny black shoes were scuffed and muddy. Now, when he marched up and down in the playroom, everyone looked at him and giggled.

Then one day, as he sat in the toy box, Soldier Bob heard a squeaky cry for help. Peering out of the window he saw a doll, called Molly. She was hanging onto the ivy growing on the wall below the playroom window. Poor Molly had been left lying on the window ledge and had fallen out. "Hold on!" called Soldier Bob, "I'm on my way!"

Leaning far out of the window he caught Molly's hand and pulled her to safety. Molly was very grateful. "However can I thank you?" she asked. "Well, you could help me smarten up my uniform," replied Bob, looking down at his tattered and muddy clothes. So, Molly happily set to work. She washed, patched, sewed and polished, and by the very next morning Soldier Bob was the smartest toy in the playroom, once again.

Dolly Talkalot

Of all the toys in the playroom, Dolly Talkalot was probably the noisiest. Whenever her string was pulled, she would say things like, "I want a nice glass of milk!" or "Dolly wants a big hug!" or "Give Dolly a kiss." or "Dolly wants a story."

At first it was fun, but the toys soon found out that she was rather difficult to talk to, because you had no idea what she was going to say in reply. You might walk up to her and say, "What a lovely, sunny day!" but Dolly Talkalot would smile and reply, "I want to go to sleep!" or "Give Dolly a big smile."

"What's the matter?" asked Eddy, but Dolly didn't say anything. They tried pulling her string, but nothing happened. "Ah ha!" said Sailor Sam, "I think I know what's wrong - her string's got stuck. Here Tiny Ted, put your little hand in there and try to loosen it up, me hearty!" he suggested.

This meant that the toys didn't talk to Dolly very much, even though she was a very nice toy. Then one day all the toys noticed that the playroom seemed very quiet for some reason. "What's going on?" said Eddy, the cuddly bunny. "It seems so quiet."
"I've no idea," said Tiny Ted, the tiny teddy. "I thought that, too."
"I know," said Sailor Sam, suddenly. "We haven't heard a single word from Dolly Talkalot all morning!"
So they went to look for Dolly and found her in the corner, crying.

Tiny Ted unstuck the string, and gave it a tug. "Are you alright?" he asked.
"Dolly wants a biscuit!"Dolly replied.
Everyone in the playroom laughed - happy to know that Dolly Talkalot was back to normal again.

The Ballerina Doll

The ballerina doll had been sleeping for many, many years. She lay cold, dusty and cobwebby in an old trunk in the attic of an old house. She had been there undisturbed for ages, until a new family moved into the house. One day the Ballerina Doll heard a voice saying, "I wonder what's in this old trunk," and then was dazzled by the light, as the creaky lid was lifted. "Aaaaah! Look!.. Look! Mother...It's a ballerina doll", gasped a little girl, as she reached in and lifted the doll out.

"Oh dear! Mmm...Needs a bit of a clean and mend," said Mother, blowing away the dust and cobwebs.

The next day the Ballerina Doll began to live again. She was cleaned, her hair was brushed and her costume washed and mended. There was just one thing missing - her ballet shoes had been lost many, many years before. They had been chewed up by a dog! "It's going to be difficult to find any that will fit her, because she's such an old doll," said Mother, "but don't worry, we'll try."

them to shape, sewed tiny pieces of pink ribbon onto them and slipped them onto the Ballerina Doll's feet one by one. They fitted perfectly, and when the ribbons were tied into bows the Ballerina Doll looked beautiful.

That night, as the little girl slept, the happy Ballerina Doll danced on her toes again, for the first time in many, many years.

Weeks and weeks went by, but they couldn't find any ballet shoes to fit the doll. They tried every toy shop in town, but no one had any that would fit. Then one day Mother called and said she had a surprise. There in her hand was a soft, white, leather glove. "I thought my doll needed shoes, not gloves," said the little girl, as she watched her mother snip the fingertips from two of the fingers. She trimmed

The Pony Trap

Penny Pony was the most beautiful toy pony anyone in the playroom had ever seen. She had big brown eyes and the longest, shiniest mane and tail you could imagine. Penny knew she was very beautiful because everyone was always telling her. She spent most of her time looking at herself in the mirror that hung on the door of her toy stable.

Every day Squeaky Sara, the doll, would come by the stable to see her. "Would you like your tail brushed, Penny?" she would ask nicely, and Penny would nod her head gracefully. Then later, the Twins would visit. "Can we brush your lovely mane?" they would ask and Penny, who loved being brushed and admired would nod gracefully again.

But one bright, sunny day something dreadful happened! The Twins were walking Penny Pony across the playroom, when Penny stopped to roll on the carpet to scratch her back.